Serenity

"Space Cadet vs. Drama Queen"

™

Includes **2** Stories

D0046981

REALBUZZ STUDIOS

E WORLD'S PREMIER INSPIRATIONAL MANGA ™

" . . . a clean, inspiring Christian comic done in a hip, contemporary way. I think you've got a real winner."

STAN LEE, co-creator of *Spider-Man*, *X-Men*, and *The Hulk*

Yeah! Like the part when that girl heard behind her --

SALLY RICHMOND!

Eeek!

What are you doing coming out of an R-rated movie?

Busted! Busted!

The stuff in the ship may be too difficult...

Not necessarily.

We can make sets and consoles outta cardboard boxes.

First we stick foam packing and other stuff to the outsides...

Then we paint it up...

stick Christmas lights inside...

And *voilá*! A sci-fi console!

I can **not** believe you just said "*voilá*!"

Hey, I scored an "A" in French!

What about all these props?

Easy! Plastic bottles, cardboard tubes, painted up junk...

I could do that...

Does this outfit make me look like I'm from outer space?

It's not the outfit that does that...

Har-dee-har-har...

Just what kinda movie **are** you making?

Relax, it's just a sci-fi movie Tim came up with.

Still...

What would you say if it **was** the wrong kinda movie?

Unless you've murdered somebody and neglected to tell me --

-- I don't think there's a lotta "wrong" you haven't tried...

You haven't, have you?

Sally can't see you. She's grounded.

DAD!

You said it was okay if it was for the youth group.

Well...

What **are** you wearing?

Costumes for the youth group project.

COOL!

Or do you think you failed to instill any values in her?

But her costume--

Her costume is unusual. It is not inappropriate.

So what do I...?

Find some face-saving way to back down.

Man, what's wrong with him?

He's always like this recently.

=Ahem!=

I've given it a little more thought, Sally.

It would be unfair to your friends to pull you out now.

I don't approve of your costume but...

...you may wear it.

??? All that drama for nuthin'?

Here's a dollar. Buy yourself a clue.

Fine, I've got the crappiest Mom on the planet. Satisfied?

Dad's not bad, he's just kinda strict.

Weird. My mom's not strict at all but she really bugs me.

If she's not strict why is she always yelling at you?

That's just it, she's not strict where it matters.

AIEEEEEE!

I'm sorry, but did I just hear you ask for limits?

NO... well... yes.... maybe in a way. Kinda.

Glad you cleared that up.

I think what I want is guidance.

I'm no prude --

-- but I want some kinda instructions.

Understatement of the Year

Wanna come in?

No, thanks!

I've seen enough parental rampages for one night.

Yeah, know what you mean.

Mom, can I ask about something you said earlier?

What?

You said, "Your body, your choice." What would **you** choose?

You're here, aren't you?

But you can't quit! Yeah, Kimberly's bossy but it's **your** movie!

Doesn't feel like it...

I know you're frustrated, but you can't quit now!

Did you guys quit on me when I acted like a butthead?

See "Bad Girl in Town"

I never thought I'd hear you encouraging me like that!

Yeah, well, you guys are starting to rub off on me!

SQUINK SQUINK SQUINK

Okay, tantrum over! Back to work!

Stop bossing Tim around...

After all, he's not your boyfriend.

Where were you? We can't waste time!

Sorry -- my bad.

Shoulda guessed...

Get in make-up for your first scene.

Hey, Mom, remember when we were talking about choices a couple of days ago...?

...yeah...?

I just want to say thanks for choosing yes seventeen years ago.

Hey, Tim! It's been two weeks! Where's the movie?

Er...it's coming.

Yeah...but when?

Soon.

He looks nervous. Maybe it didn't turn out as he hoped.

Who cares? I'm impressed he did it!

He's a perfectionist. He'll never show it until he's ready...

...but the thing is, he'll never be ready!

Then we just gotta arrange our own sneak preview!

WHAT'S A KLAPPON ESCAPE POD DOING IN THIS SECTOR?

THEY'RE NOTORIOUS FOR SENDING SCOUTING PROBES INTO OUR TERRITORY.

BUT THIS COULD BE A SHIP THAT JUST DRIFTED OFF COURSE...

WE WON'T KNOW UNTIL WE FIND IT.

GREAT! YOU FOUND MY BANANA CLIP!

WHAT HAPPENED TO IT?

SCIENCE OFFICER, GO ABOARD AND CHECK IT OUT.

ME?

YOU'RE WEARING A RED SHIRT, AREN'T YOU?

AYE-AYE, SIR!

CYCLING

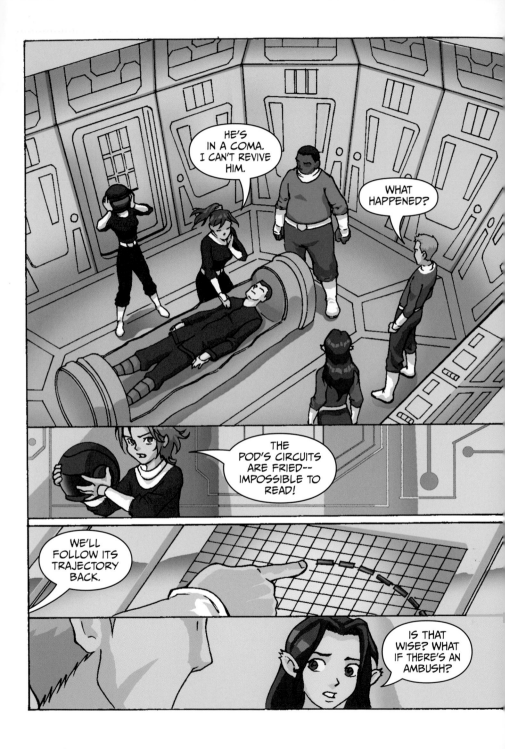

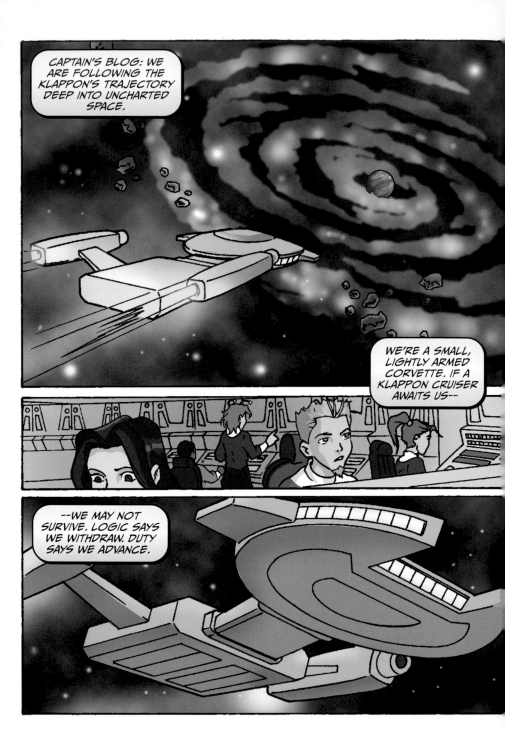

WE'VE LOCATED THE SYSTEM WHERE THE KLAPPON POD ORIGINATED!

IT CAME FROM AN EARTH-LIKE PLANET. NO SIGNS OF TECHNOLOGY.

CAN WE SCAN THE SURFACE?

NEGATIVE. HIDDEN BY CLOUDS.

RADAR INDICATES POSSIBLE RUINS-- WAIT! PICKING UP A KLAPPON HOMING SIGNAL!

SEND A RESPONSE.

NO RESPONSE-- IT SEEMS TO BE AUTOMATED.

THEN FOLLOW IT IN.

ATTENTION CREW--PREPARE TO LAND!

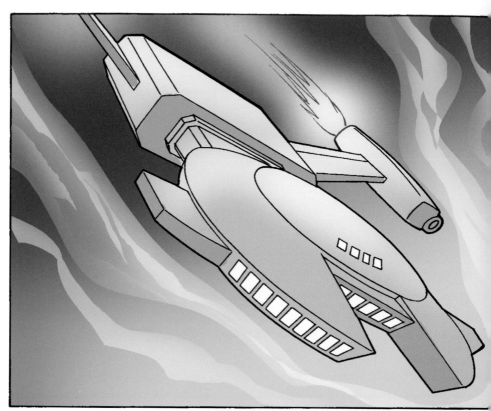

FIRE DOWN BELOW--
BETTER LAND
QUICKLY!

THERE!
LAND IN THAT
CLEARING!

DAMAGE REPORT!

THE FIRE'S OUT BUT I'LL NEED TO INSPECT THE DRIVE!

TAKE A PARTY OUT TO SCOUT THE PERIMETER.

AYE-AYE, SIR.

YEAH, YEAH, I KNOW. "RED SHIRT" AGAIN...

ANY SIGN OF CIVILIZA- TION?

YES, SIR. I THINK YOU CAN SAY THAT...

WHAT'S THE DAMAGE?

FULL ACCOUNTING OR BOTTOM LINE?

BOTTOM LINE.

BROKEN, BUT WE CAN FIX IT.

HOW'S THE KLAPPON?

STILL COMATOSE.

ODD... THAT FORCE FIELD GREW STRONGER THE CLOSER WE GOT TO THE PLANET...

WHILE WE'RE REPAIRING THE SHIP, INVESTIGATE THAT ALIEN FORTRESS.

AYE-AYE, SIR.

COME WITH ME. I'LL NEED YOU IF WE ENCOUNTER ANY ALIEN LANGUAGES.

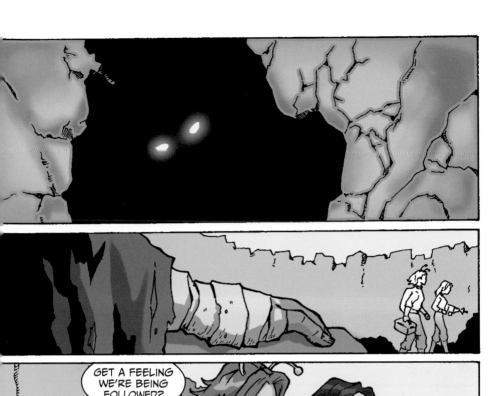

GET A FEELING WE'RE BEING FOLLOWED?

I KNOW WE'RE BEING FOLLOWED.

METEOR?

NO--IT'S A NUCLEAR BOMB CRATER, BUT THOUSANDS OF YEARS OLD.

DON'T HURT THEM!

I'M TRYING NOT TO--

--BUT THEY MAY NOT GIVE US MUCH CHOICE!

CAN WE LAUNCH THE SHUTTLE?

NEGATIVE, SIR--THAT'S WHERE THE FIRE STARTED!

WHAT ABOUT THE LAND CRAWLER?

IT'LL TAKE AN HOUR TO GET READY.

I WANT IT READY IN FIFTEEN MINUTES!

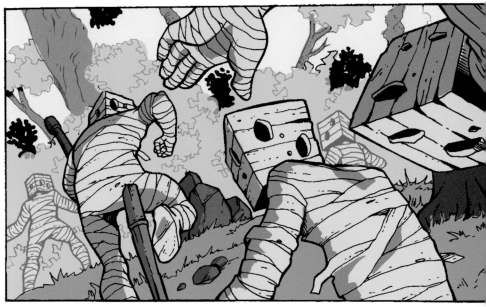

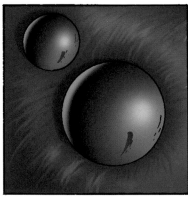

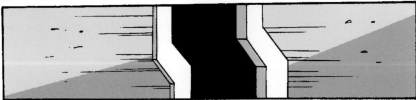

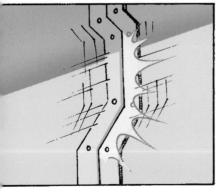

WHO ARE YOU? WHAT ARE THOSE THINGS OUTSIDE?

MY NAME IS PRINCESS ANYAMA. I'LL EXPLAIN THE REST IN MY CHAMBERS.

WE FOLLOWED A KLAPPON SIGNAL HERE.

I DO NOT KNOW THESE "KLAPPONS." IF THEY LANDED HERE THEY NEVER REACHED ME.

I'M TRAPPED ALL ALONE ON THIS WORLD--TAKE ME WITH YOU!

WE'RE NOT GOING ANYWHERE UNTIL THE RESCUE PARTY REACHES US!

WE DON'T HAVE TO WAIT! THE PLATFORMS CAN TAKE US TO YOUR SHIP!

I'M GETTING A READING NOW THAT WE'RE OUT OF THE FORTRESS.

THE KLAPPON SHIP IS JUST OVER THE HORIZON.

THANK YOU.

...AH... ALLOW ME TO SHOW YOU THE SHIP...

SHE KILLED MY CAPTAIN AND TRIED TO LAUNCH THE SHIP.

WE SABOTAGED THE DRIVE BUT SHE STARTED KILLING US. ONLY I ESCAPED.

EXACTLY WHAT WERE YOU DOING IN THIS SECTOR ANYWAY?

...URM... NAVIGATION ERROR...WE TOOK A WRONG TURN AT ALDEBARAN...

JUST A LITTLE MORE TIME! I FOUND SOME IMPORTANT DATA!

NEGATIVE! RETURN NOW!

ROGER-- BUT KEEP AN EYE ON PRINCESS ANYAMA!

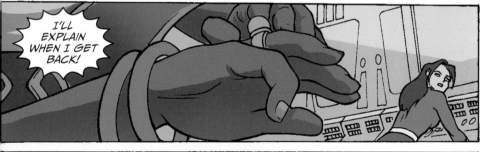

I'LL EXPLAIN WHEN I GET BACK!

!!!

THE POWER!

...OH... SNAP...

CAPTAIN! THE SCIENCE OFFICER HAS BEEN CAPTURED BY MUTANTS!

WARM UP THE CRAWLER AND ORGANIZE A RESCUE PARTY IMMEDIATELY!

I'M AFRAID IT'S USELESS. IF THE MUTANTS GOT HER, SHE'S DEAD!

NO, SHE'S NOT! WE'RE STILL GETTING A LIFE READING FROM HER!

BREAK OUT THE BLASTERS-- WE'LL GO ON FOOT!

NO! I FORBID IT!

STAY BEHIND THE CONTROLS--SHE DOESN'T WANT TO DAMAGE THE SHIP!

DISTRACT HER AND I'LL INJECT HER WITH A UNIVERSAL SEDATIVE!

PSSSST

STRANGE-- THESE AREN'T HIBERNATION UNITS! THESE BODIES AREN'T ALIVE!

THEY'RE DECOYS DESIGNED TO LOOK LIKE FEMALES OF VARIOUS SPECIES!

THEY'RE MEANT TO APPEAR ATTRACTIVE.

YOU WEREN'T ATTACKING EARLIER, WERE YOU? YOU WERE TRYING TO WARN US...

SCIENCE OFFICER TO CAPTAIN--YOU NEED TO WATCH OUT FOR THE PRINCESS!

THANKS FOR THE WARNING...

WHEN I HEARD THE FIGHT, I KNEW THE FEMALE HAD RETURNED.

I "BORROWED" THE LASER WELDER FROM ENGINEERING AS A WEAPON...

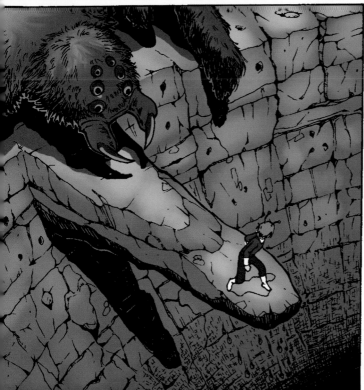

IF YOU DON'T JUMP I'LL EAT YOU ALIVE!

WAIT-- SOMETHING'S NOT RIGHT HERE!

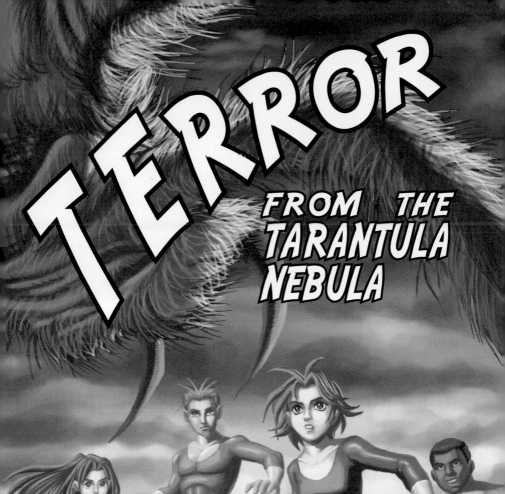

TERROR

FROM THE TARANTULA NEBULA

starring:

KIMBERLY CALVIN   DEREK ANGSTROM   SERENITY HARPER   TIM PATTERSON

Written.Produced.Directed
by
TIM PATTERSON

How We Made
"TERROR FROM THE TARANTULA NEBULA"
by
Serenity Harper (Class 6a)

Okay, so the deal is this: Mr. Pyle said if I do extra credit work he will raise my F to a D- and if I have a D- in English then I don't hafta take summer school.

have to

use brackets inside parenthesis

So I'm going to write about the movies we're making (we as in Derek *YUM* and me and Lori and Sally and all the rest) (yes, including Kimberly).

So Tim had this idea for a sci-fi movie and the first thing he axed me is if he can *asked* blow Tinkerbelle up and I said,"You are so NOT going to put firecrackers anywhere near Tinkerbelle!!!" and he saiod no, use trick photography to make her look big. *Only one exclamation point!!!*

Stay consistent when using quotes!

So we built this little dinky set that was supposed to be the alien princess' home and we put Tinkerbelle in there and she acted just like a pro! Then Tim had me stand in front of an old green sheet and pretend I was running and when he put it all together in the computer it looked like Tinkerbelle was a giant and she was chasing me! Atta girl, Tink! *Run on sentence!*

For other scenes he would do stuff like put a little model of the spaceship in front of the camera then have us stand about 20 or 30 feet back only when you looked through the camera it seemed like the ship was big and we were right next to it.

Need more detail!

Okay, that's a page. Only 3 more to go! Yippeeee!

C-ya!

C-ren

We heard the call...

Hey!
Serenity
Where did
you go
?!?!?

...and here she is!

Refreshed art!

Restored dialog!

Brand new covers!

Same ol' Serenity!

Don't miss any of her
new re-releases from
Thomas Nelson!
"Bad Girl In Town"
"Stepping Out"
"Basket Case"
"Rave and Rant"
"Snow Biz"
"You Shall Love..."

Find her
=oof!=
in stores
=grunt!=
now!

I sure
hope her
books
aren't
this
heavy!

Don't worry,
they're light
reading...

Life's a beach --
come and play!

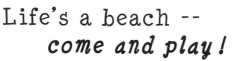

"INSANELY UNIQUE!"
-- MangaPunk.com

You can find
anything on a beach
-- especially FUN
and ROMANCE!

Making her splash in stores now!
LET THERE BE LIGHTEN UP! ▪ WHEN DOLPHINS FLY
COME AND PLAY! ▪ OUT OF THE SOUP
Created by Realbuzz Studios
Published by Thomas Nelson
Find out more at
www.RealbuzzStudios.com
www.GoofyfootGurl.com

iT'S
LIFE !
CAMERA !
ACTION !
starring
Serenity
™

Serenity is back with
ALL NEW STORIES
that mix humor, heartache,
homework & just a touch of
Hollywood hoopla as she
and her friends start
making their own brand of
off-beat movies !

ALL THE SASS & TWICE THE **FUN!**

Don't miss these great new
titles from Thomas Nelson
& Realbuzz Studios !

"Space Cadet vs. Drama Queen"
"Sunday Best"
"Choosing Change"
"Girl Overboard"

MAKE THE JUMP TO OUR WEBSITES !

www.SerenityBuzz.com
www.GoofyfootGurl.com
and
www.RealbuzzStudios.com not only talk about
Serenity and the Prayer Club but also upcoming new
series from Thomas Nelson and Realbuzz Studios like
GOOFYFOOT GURL and many, **many more !**

Make sure you visit us regularly
for advance news, fun facts, downloads, contests
and challenges, as well as online shopping !

Can you make a video ?
Do you have a recipe ?

Exciting new contests
coming soon to
www.RealbuzzStudios.com !

Looking For

Serenity™ Swag

Or

Goofyfoot™ Gear ?

Check out our online shop at
www.RealbuzzStudios.com
www.SerenityBuzz.com
www.GoofyfootGurl.com
www.GoofyfootGuy.com
[Protoypes shown; final product may differ slightly.]

Serenity

Created by Realbuzz Studios, Inc.
Min Kwon, Primary Artist
Studio Sakai, Collaborative Art

Serenity throws a big wet sloppy one out to:
The captains & crews of the Enterprise, the Yamato, and Fireball XL-5
Smack!
Luv U Guyz !!!

©&TM 2007 by Realbuzz Studios   ISBN 1-59554-394-5 / 978-1-59554-394-3
www.RealbuzzStudios.com
www.SerenityBuzz.com

All rights reserved. No part of this publication may be reproduced or transmitted for commercial purposes, except for brief quotations in printed reviews, without written permission of the publisher.

This book is a work of fiction. Names, characters, places, and incidents are either products of the author's imagination or used fictitiously. Any similarity to actual people, organizations, and/or events is purely coincidental.

Published by Thomas Nelson, Inc. Nashville, TN 37214 www.thomasnelson.com

Library of Congress Cataloguing-in-Publication Data
Applied For

Scripture quotations marked NCV are taken from
The HOLY BIBLE, New Century VERSION®. NCV®.
Copyright © 2001 by Nelson Bibles.
Used by permission of Thomas Nelson. All rights reserved.

Printed in Singapore.
5 4 3 2 1